Third Edition

pale as the moon

By Donna Campbell Smith

Faithful Publishing
Buford, Georgia

Published by:
Faithful Publishing
PO Box 345
Buford, GA 30515

Third Printing Copyright ©2006 by Donna Campbell Smith
ISBN: 0-9759941-6-6 (10 digit)
        978-09759941-6-0 (13 digit)

First Printing Copyright ©1999 by Donna Campbell
Second Printing Copyright ©2000 by Donna Campbell

Illustrations by Debi Davis - www.debidavisart.com

Originally published by Coastal Carolina Press - ISBN 1-928556-02-7
Printed in the United States of America

Publisher's Cataloging-In-Publication Data
(Prepared by The Donohue Group, Inc.)

Campbell, Donna, 1946-
    Pale as the moon / Donna Campbell Smith. -- 3rd ed.

    p. : ill., map ; cm. + 1 study guide.

    ISBN-13: 978-0-9759941-6-0 (pbk.)
    ISBN-10: 0-9759941-6-6 (pbk.)
    Includes bibliographical references.
    Summary: On visits to the sandy Outer Banks islands off the coast of North Carolina, a
sixteenth-century Paspatank girl named Gray Squirrel befriends a wild pony, and together they
fulfill their destiny of helping the English colonists on Roanoke Island.

    1. Roanoke Colony--Juvenile fiction. 2. Indians of North America--North Carolina--Juvenile
fiction. 3. Roanoke Colony--Fiction. 4. Indians of North America--North Carolina--Fiction. 5.
Ponies--Fiction. 6. America--
Discovery and exploration--English--Fiction. I. Title.

PZ7.C15097 Pal 2006
813.54   2006922535

To Mama, who taught me about faith and hope, and Daddy, who taught me to love books and to dream.

Thank you.

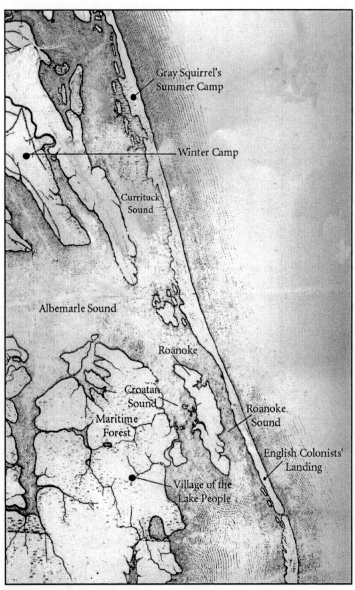

Outer Banks of North Carolina
Map courtesy of the Department of Cultural Resources, Division of Archives & History
Raleigh, North Carolina

Table of Contents

Chapter One

1582

A cold February wind blew across the sandy island, making even the dried sea oats shiver. Gray, angry waves pounded the ocean's shore and only a few brave sea gulls flew low to catch whatever hapless minnows didn't wash back out to sea.

On the western shore of the island, a stand of bent and twisted oak trees sheltered a small herd of horses. One of them, a little bay colt, huddled close to his mother and nuzzled her flank, searching for the warm milk from her teats. His forehead was marked with a white half-moon.

It was a harsh world into which this little horse had been born. His home was one of stormy winds and scorching heat. His only foods were wild sea grasses and shrubs, and he had to dig in the sand for pools of brackish water. Food was harder to find in winter. He and his herd survived on the brown, tough grass which grew in the salt marshes.

Spring came early to the mid-Atlantic coast. The

youngster became strong and swift as he played in the surf with the other colts. His hooves barely touched the ground as he trotted across the deep sand. He frolicked in the huge waves that washed sand out from under his hooves as he galloped along the shore.

In the simmering heat of summer, the horses often had to wade into the water to escape the mosquitoes and gnats which came in thick, black clouds with the inland breezes. Afternoon showers and thunderstorms brought some relief, cooling the air and leaving pools of fresh water for them to drink.

The colts played games of chase and hide-and-seek among the weathered oak trees. The little bay stopped occasionally and peered from under the moss-laden trees to make sure his mother was still close by. If he strayed too far she always whinnied loudly, telling him to come back.

The summer heat intensified, and the late August night offered no relief. The herd was restless. They gathered close to the woods on the Sound side of the island. There was no breeze, and the mosquitoes were hungry. The horses stomped and shook their heads, trying to rid themselves of the bloodthirsty insects. Some of the youngsters broke into a gallop, trying to flee their tormentors, but the mosquitoes could not be outrun. As dawn broke, the mares tightened the group and moved closer to the woods.

The colt sensed a peculiar smell in the air. His nostrils flared and he snorted, trying to identify the odor. It was more than the dry, scorching smell of the sand and sea grass.

The sky began to fill with black clouds, and the

wind grew stronger. The colt had experienced storms before, but he could feel this was different. He noticed others in the herd becoming restless.

His mother whinnied shrilly at him and, nipping at his rear, guided him to a cluster of trees behind the sand dunes. The wind roared and the rain fell in great sheets. Long, jagged fingers of lightning streaked across the sky. Trembling with fear, the yearling leaned against his mother for comfort, holding his head down and ears flat against the driving rain. Never had the wind blown with such mighty force.

When lightning hit a nearby tree, splitting it in two, the colt reared and pawed at the sky. He wheeled around to run, but his mother whinnied for him to stay, knowing safety lay with the herd. Broken branches and leaves were tossed through the air. The young colt had never been so frightened. He stood close to his mother, legs quivering.

Suddenly, lightning hit another tree. The tree exploded, and a burning branch fell across his back, searing the hair and burning into his flesh. This time he did run, despite his mother's protests. He ran as fast as his legs would go. He forgot the herd, and thought only about escaping the pain.

The wind howled louder. He didn't hear his mother's call. Sand blew in great blinding swirls which stung like a swarm of bees. The colt kept running and running until he was exhausted. Finally he dropped down in the sand, too weak to move. He lay there, trembling. The rain poured harder.

The storm stopped as suddenly as it had begun. Blue sky replaced the angry black clouds. The surf no longer pounded the beach. Now the ocean was smooth, with only a small ripple lapping at the shoreline. The only clues that a hurricane had passed were the uprooted trees and litter of broken limbs and leaves covering the sand. A deep channel of water now cut the island in two.

The sun warmed the drenched body of the little colt. He woke and looked around for the herd. Tired and hungry, he stood up and whinnied for his mother. There was no answer. He called and called. He began to trot frantically in circles, searching for the other horses. By nightfall the colt, cold and hungry, collapsed at the foot of a sand dune.

By morning hunger pains replaced his urgency to find the herd. He wandered further south, nibbling the grass that grew along the Sound side of the island. He stopped several times, listening intently for his mother's call. When he was sure the sound he heard was only the wind whistling through the reeds, he continued eating.

By midmorning the heat was intense, and the colt found a patch of myrtle bushes for shade. He was lying down, resting, when a noise alerted him. Twitching an ear and shaking his head to get rid of an irritating fly, he listened. The noise wasn't the nickering or whinny of horses, or the surf lapping at the beach. It wasn't the gulls laughing.

This was a new sound.

He stood up, holding his head high, and he twitched his ears back and forth to determine the sound's direction. He concentrated his ears and his gaze toward the marsh. Yes, something was moving through the grass!

Chapter Two

Gray Squirrel heard the colt's loud whinnying and walked out of the marsh toward the clump of myrtle bushes. At first the large dark mass looked like a bear, but the young Paspatank girl knew bears did not sound like that. She watched and moved closer. Now she could see that it was a horse.

The colt stood motionless. She could feel his huge dark eyes fixed on her. She bent over to snatch a handful of grass. Arm outstretched with her offering, she stepped a bit closer, but when she took another step the horse tossed his head, turned, and galloped over the dunes and out of sight.

Gray Squirrel's grandmother, White Deer, called, "What are you doing? Come help me gather more thatch. There will be time to play after we are done."

The girl obediently rejoined the group and began cutting more grass.

"Did you see him?" Gray Squirrel pointed where the colt had been standing. "Did you hear him? He sounded so afraid. Where do you think the rest of his family is? Why was he without his mother?"

"He will find his way back." White Deer spoke softly. "Think of him no more. We have much work to do to rebuild our wickiup."

Gray Squirrel felt sad for the little colt, lost and motherless. She too had been separated from her mother, who had died when Gray Squirrel was just a baby. Though she missed her mother, she loved White Deer with all of her heart. Her grandmother was an important woman in their town. She had knowledge of healing herbs, and her wisdom earned her honor and esteem among all of the Paspatank people.

The hurricane had destroyed most of the Paspatank's camp. Gray Squirrel knew they were very fortunate that no one had been injured. She had taken refuge with her grandmother under an overturned dugout canoe.

Her bundle was heavy as she carried it back to the site, but Gray Squirrel hardly noticed. All she could think about was the bay colt. She had seen horses before, but never one this close.

She had heard many stories about how horses came to live on these islands. They were left there long ago by strangers who had come looking for gold and precious stones. She would ask her grandfather, Black Feather, to tell the stories again tonight.

The barrier islands were not the permanent home of the Paspatank. Their town was further inland. Gray Squirrel had come with her family to fish and dry the catch in the sun to preserve it for the winter.

During the summer, they cast long nets into the ocean and together pulled them in, heavy with many fish. The fish were cut into thin strips and hung on drying racks. When they'd caught and dried enough, the tribe moved back to the main village.

☽

By late afternoon, the repairs to the camp were completed and the family ate their supper.

"Tell me about the horses, Grandfather!" Gray Squirrel loved the stories Black Feather told around the evening fire.

"They were brought here many years ago, in the days when your father was about your age," Black Feather began. "Men came in great boats from across the ocean.

Their skin was very light, and they dressed in colorful garments and had frightening and powerful weapons. The men brought swine and cattle for food, but they did not eat the horses. Horses were their brothers, and carried the men from place to place. This was how the horses shared their strength and speed.

"These men searched for gold and precious stones. They were greedy and cruel people. When they could not find the riches they wanted, they kidnapped our children and sold them for slaves. Your mother's sister was one of those children. She was never seen again after the white men took her.

"The tribal councils met and warriors came from all over the land to drive the bad men back to their ships. They sailed away in such fear that they left their animals behind. The horses still roam the islands to the north."

"I saw one today," Gray Squirrel exclaimed. "He must be separated from his mother. I heard him crying and could see the fear in his eyes. Grandfather, I want this horse to be my brother and carry me like the wind." The words tumbled out of Gray Squirrel like a waterfall.

Black Feather looked amused. "The horses are wild like the deer. You will never get close enough to climb on that young one's back. Enough storytelling, child. Go to sleep."

Sleep was slow in coming to the little girl. Her thoughts were filled with plans about how to win the trust of the dark colt with the half-moon on his forehead. When she finally fell asleep, she dreamed of him whinnying from the top of the tall sand dunes. Tomorrow she would find this horse that called to her in the wind.

Chapter Three

The women were up at dawn to tend the fires under the drying racks.

Gray Squirrel and the other children played games, but after a while she wandered away from her playmates. She climbed over the dunes where the colt had disappeared the day before. She had an ear of dried corn, and she pulled up shoots of tender grass along the way. She moved quietly, her eyes searching the seascape for the colt.

Soon she found hoofprints in the wet sand along the shore, but the little horse was not in sight. She followed the prints, but when she reached the dunes again, the wind had erased them.

She sat down near the top and hid among the sea oats. The dry tops rattled softly in the wind. Suddenly she heard another sound. When she turned in the direction of the noise, she saw him. He was digging in the sand with his hooves. Soon the hole he made filled with water, and he began to drink.

Gray Squirrel moved silently down the dune,

still hidden by the tall grass. She waited patiently until he finished drinking. Then she crawled closer and spoke in a low voice: "It is me. I have food." She laid the corn and grass near the water hole and backed away as slowly as she had approached.

The colt stared with curiosity at this strange creature. He didn't feel threatened, but still he was cautious. He stared until she was out of sight before he walked over to the pile of grass.

His ears were alert, straining to hear any sound of movement. Finally he nibbled at the grass. Then he discovered the corn. It smelled good. He took a bite—it was good. He greedily ate the corn and scattered the grass looking for more.

He didn't notice the girl sitting on top of the sand dune, watching.

Gray Squirrel visited the dunes every day and left food for the colt. Each day she sat a little closer to the water hole, until she could stay in plain sight without scaring him away.

The colt was not so afraid anymore. He expected the food and especially looked forward to the corn.

One morning, Gray Squirrel woke up filled with excitement. "Today I will touch this beautiful creature," she told the wind. "I will wait for him to eat out of my hand and he will thank me, knowing I mean him no harm."

The little girl was anxious to meet the colt face to face, and her heart beat quickly. She moved quietly through the grassy dunes. When she reached the water hole, she sat in the sand and placed the grass and the ear of corn in her lap. She waited.

Gray Squirrel felt the colt watching her, but she sat still and resisted the urge to turn around and look. Then she heard him walk slowly toward her.

He waited.

She could see him now, standing to her left side, watching her with big, dark eyes. He was ready to run the moment he felt threatened.

"Come closer, see what I brought you?" Gray Squirrel slowly held out the ear of corn. "Come on, I won't hurt you. One day we will run together with the wind."

The colt snorted and shook his head, then

lowered it. He stepped closer. Gray Squirrel held her breath and didn't move a muscle. Then the colt stretched his neck out and sniffed the corn.

Quickly he grabbed the corn in his teeth and stepped back a little. He ate the food, still watching the little girl. When he finished she spoke to him again. "Ah, look! I have more. But you must let me touch you to earn the second ear."

This time Gray Squirrel did not hold the corn out to him, but held it close to her lap.

The colt hesitated a moment before reaching down for the corn. When he did, Gray Squirrel slid her hand under his mane and felt his warm neck. She could smell the sea and the warm sun-smell of his dark coat. She felt the smoothness of his muscles.

The colt stopped munching and looked at her.

He didn't run away.

At that instant, Gray Squirrel felt their spirits bond.

Chapter Four

Summer would soon come to an end. Already the days were shorter and the nights pleasantly cool.

Gray Squirrel continued to visit the water hole and feed the colt. She combed his long mane and tail and talked softly while he ate. She walked alongside him as he grazed among the marshes. When the mosquitoes became more than either of them could bear, they walked into the shallows until they were submerged up to their necks.

Every night Gray Squirrel dreamed of the bay colt with the half-moon on his forehead. In her dreams he carried her on his back and galloped along the ocean's shore. Waves rolled high and crashed around his flint-black hooves. She could feel the salty spray in her face as they flew like the wind, the colt's courage overflowing into her heart. She called him Heita Hoonoch—Moon Wind.

One morning, the distant rumble of thunder woke Gray Squirrel. By daybreak, clouds moved in from the ocean and raindrops began to fall. The Paspatank would not fish today. The women would use this time to mend nets and repair and make new baskets.

Gray Squirrel knew she would be expected to help, but she longed to see the colt. When she missed a day, she worried that he would not wait for her, but always he was at the water hole or close by. She had learned to mimic his whinny, which always brought him galloping to her side.

"Soon we will return home." White Deer spoke as they sat on the floor of their wickiup, weaving reeds into strong baskets. "Our work here is almost done. The sea has been generous with her gifts."

Gray Squirrel's heart sank. She had not thought of leaving.

"Grandmother, when will we go?"

"In a few days," White Deer answered.

Gray Squirrel worked silently, thinking. The Currituck Sound separated the summer camp and their inland village. The Paspatank would paddle their dugout canoes across the sound to a wide river. From there they would travel up the river to their village. It was a long journey. There was no way to take the colt home.

"I know what you are thinking, child," White Deer said, "but it will not be wise to take Heita Hoonoch back to the village. Even if he can swim across the Sound, he might not be well received by those who will remember where he came from. And if the winter is hard, we will not be able to spare food for him. In fact, he might be considered food, by some."

Gray Squirrel knew her grandmother spoke with wisdom, and so she did not argue. The tribe would return in the spring. Then she and Heita Hoonoch would be reunited.

By afternoon, the sky cleared and the families moved to outside activities. Gray Squirrel, finished with her tasks, slipped away from the other children, taking an ear of corn with her. She reached the water hole and saw the colt grazing in the sea oats down the beach.

Standing at the top of a dune, she whinnied loudly. Heita Hoonoch threw his head up in recognition and whinnied back, then galloped toward her.

Her heart beat fast as she offered him the corn. "Listen, my friend, we have only a little time left before I must return to the village with my family. I will have to go without you. But I will come back when the grass comes up green and the herring month is past."

Gray Squirrel's face was wet with tears as she ran her hand across the colt's neck and grasped his mane. He twitched an ear and shook his head at the cloud of gnats that hovered around his face.

"While I am gone you must stay safe. Do not forget me," she instructed. Then she turned and ran back to the camp.

He came again in her dreams that night. While she lay asleep, he nudged her and blew his breath softly on her cheek. Her dream spirit rose up. With her fingers intertwined in his mane, she sprang lightly onto his back.

The colt reared and lunged forward. He galloped down the beach, his hooves flashing in the moonlight. Suddenly Gray Squirrel realized they were flying. She looked down and watched the campfires disappear. They soared above the ocean with the moon and stars to light their way.

Heita Hoonoch slowed and they glided in the air like a leaf caught in the breeze.

A curious object appeared below them, bobbing on the waves. It looked like a huge white bird with its wings spread, about to take flight. Gray Squirrel and her mount swooped down closer. She saw that it was not a bird at all, but a boat—a boat bigger than any she had seen before. It had great white sails and moved swiftly across the ocean.

Voices from the deck of the ship, spoken in a strange language, carried easily across the silent vastness of the sea.

"Closer, go closer. I want to see these people," she whispered.

The colt glided up to the ship's side.

Gray Squirrel's heart stopped a moment in fear. The men were dressed in odd, brightly colored skins, but that was not what frightened her. It was their faces! Their faces were as pale as the moon that shone in the black sky.

"Quick, please take me back." Gray Squirrel's voice trembled with fear and she clenched the horse's mane tighter.

Heita Hoonoch spun quickly on his haunches and they soared back up into the clouds. Soon there was only the blackness of the sea mingled with that of the sky.

Gray Squirrel shivered in her sleep and drew the deerskin blanket tighter around her shoulders.

A light rain fell from a sunless sky as the next day dawned. Gray Squirrel heard her grandmother rustling quietly about. White Deer was packing for the journey home while a cornmeal soup simmered in the clay cooking pot. Today they would start back to the main village.

Memories of the dream sent new chills down Gray Squirrel's back. The white faces of the men in the boat reminded her of the stories Black Feather told about the strangers who had come to their land long ago.

Chapter Five

At first Heita Hoonoch came to the water hole every day. After many days of looking for the girl, he began to move further down the beach.

There was no more green grass, only the tough, brown sea oats. Sometimes he'd nibble on leaves in the woods. Pine needles were tasty; other leaves were bitter and he left them alone.

As winter storms grew harsher, Heita Hoonoch took shelter in the woods on the Sound side of the island. His thick and shaggy winter hair kept him warm even though he was getting thin.

The colt longed for the security of the herd. The channel which separated them was even deeper and wider, washed out by more storms. The strong current which surged through it made swimming across impossible.

The cold had been interrupted by a few days of warmth, but this morning the sky was full of gray clouds. The wind began to blow and the air turned cold. By afternoon it was snowing and the wind was blowing with a vengeance. It snowed all through the night.

The next day the sun was shining again, but the beach was covered by a white blanket. Heita Hoonoch had never seen snow before. When his hooves sank through the drifts, he was startled. Whinnying, he picked up his knees higher and hopped up, only to sink to his chest in an even deeper drift.

Then he decided to explore the white stuff by nibbling at it and decided it was good, a source of fresh water as it melted on his tongue.

Navigating got easier with practice and soon he was trotting along the Sound's shore with comical animation. After a while he gained enough confidence to go galloping down the beach, bucking and kicking and scaring a group of sea gulls that were sunning themselves.

A shallow puddle, frozen solid, brought Heita Hoonoch's frolicking to a sudden stop. When his snow-packed hooves hit the ice, they slid out from under him. He scrambled to get up, but just kept slipping. Finally he got enough traction in the snow to stand. When he put his weight on his left front hoof, a burning pain shot up his leg.

Heita Hoonoch was afraid to move, afraid of the pain and afraid of losing his footing again. So, for hours, he just stood there, balancing precariously on three legs.

The sun began to set behind the Sound, casting a golden-pink hue over the snow. He shivered and ventured a few steps, but the going was slow. The pain of putting any weight on his injured foreleg was unbearable. He lay down in a thicket of reeds.

☽

Gray Squirrel and the village children played in the snow, squealing with delight. It was rare for snow to cover the ground this deeply.

The children hardly felt the freezing air. They were dressed warmly in their buckskins, with the fur side in. When they did get chilled, they'd run into their houses to sit by the fire and eat.

White Deer kept a large pot of stew simmering over the fire. The mixture of meat, corn, beans, and potatoes was thickened with cornmeal and seasoned with herbs.

"Mmm, this is good." Gray Squirrel smacked her lips in appreciation.

"We were very blessed to have such bounty in the gathering season," replied her grandmother. "I think winter will be long."

"Oh, I hope not," Gray Squirrel said. "I hope summer comes soon, so we can return to the island. I dream of Heita Hoonoch almost every night."

She took her bowl outside, cleaned it in the snow and returned it to the fireside. Then she went back outdoors, but she didn't feel like playing anymore and soon came back into the house. She lay down beside the fire and fell asleep.

Heita Hoonoch came to her in a dream, but not galloping with the wind as he had so many times before.

Instead he hobbled on three legs, holding his left foreleg off the ground. He was thin and his eyes had lost their fire. The horse whinnied so softly Gray Squirrel could hardly hear him above the crashing of the waves.

She woke up crying.

White Deer came to her. "Shhh, my little one. What is wrong, are you sick?"

"He came to me in my dream. He is hurt and starving," Gray Squirrel cried. "Oh, Grandmother, I am afraid he will die before I can see him again."

Chapter Six
1584

The winter passed slowly for Gray Squirrel. Heita Hoonoch did not visit her again in her dreams.

Finally, flowers and grass appeared. It was time to plant, and that meant it was time for the spring corn festival. There would be a huge feast and dancing. The people would give thanks for last year's bounty and pray for the coming year to yield as well. This was also a time for the people to forgive each other any wrongs they might have done.

The day of the festival arrived. The men hunted while the women and girls prepared the food. Potatoes roasted in the coals and pots of stew simmered over the fires. White Deer made little sweet cakes from the dried berries and fruit they had left. All day, while the food was prepared, the children chased each other and played games.

Soon visitors from neighboring towns began to arrive. They came from as far away as the towns of the Moraroc and Hatteras. Okisco, Manteo, Wanchese and many other important elders were among the visitors. They brought goods to trade and would take council with Great Hawk and the other chiefs of the Paspatank to discuss important matters.

The hunters had done well. Black Feather was greeted with shouts of admiration when he returned from the hunt carrying the carcass of a large, fat deer across his shoulders. By afternoon the village was filled with the aroma of roasting meat. People ate all day, sampling dishes as they finished cooking. The men told many stories, bragging about their success as hunters and warriors.

When night came, everyone gathered for the ritual dance.

The priest, Great Hawk, stood before the people and began to pray. "We the people of Paspatank come to you with gratitude and a humble spirit. We thank you for the great bounty you have given us. The corn was planted and yielded much. The sea gave us fish to feed our whole people. Our hunters have been successful. And we have lived with all our brothers in this land for many years in peace. For all this we thank you."

Then Great Hawk turned toward the young men grouped around him. "You are to continue working hard. It pleases Creator who takes care of us. It is through you that he has blessed the Paspatank with bounty and with peace.

"We come to you as your children, and so we ask you to once again pour your blessing on the People's planting and on the fruits of the earth. Give us wisdom that we may understand the lessons you have taught us. Help us respect each other and every creature that we may continue to share the earth and live in peace."

When Great Hawk finished his prayer there was a long silence. Then the dance began. The people gathered around the totem, which symbolized a messenger to the corn god. About thirty men and women, leaders of distinction, started to dance in a circle around the figure. Musicians played the rhythm on drums and rattles. Then all of the people crowded around the dancers.

White Deer was the first woman to enter the circle. She was regal in the way she moved. Even though her hair was streaked with the silver of age, she was beautiful. Her eyes spoke of wisdom and serenity. She danced in the circle of life softly, so as not to bruise Mother Earth. Her head held high, she draped her shawl over her shoulders. It was fashioned of deerskin and decorated with shell beads and feathers. It hung to her knees, and its long fringe swayed with the rhythm of the music.

Gray Squirrel felt great pride watching her grandmother dance. She felt gratitude that this woman, who was so revered among the Paspatank, loved and cared for her. Gray Squirrel prayed that she too would some day have the wisdom and knowledge that her grandmother possessed.

Before entering the circle to dance, Gray Squirrel offered a prayer of her own. "I come to you in humble thankfulness for giving me life. In my dreams I have seen my brother who runs with the wind. I have seen him injured and starving. I beg that you protect and nourish him. I beg that you spare his life and re-unite us when we return to the islands. I pray that you keep him safe until we can again climb the dunes and dance in the waves with the sea gulls. In this spirit of

gratitude I promise to serve the purpose you have for me, and I will dance for you."

The dancers danced all night. By daybreak everyone had dropped exhausted and soaked with sweat—all but the young girl, who danced on without stopping until the moon sank behind the tall pines and the sun cast its first glow on a new day. Finally, she too collapsed.

Gray Squirrel's dream spirit came over her like the fog that rolls in over a marsh on a fall morning. Through the fog, she could see an image coming toward her—but the mist grew thicker and she could not tell what it was. It came closer and loomed dark like a shadow. Soon the shadow stood next to her body.

Gray Squirrel was not afraid. She felt a familiar connection to this figure. Then she knew, as he stretched down his head and blew his breath softly upon her face: It was Heita Hoonoch.

She sat up and wrapped her arms around his neck. She buried her face in his long, shaggy mane and smelled the warm musty scent of his fur.

"You are well, my friend. Creator has answered my prayer." The girl stood up and examined the colt from head to tail. "Yes, you look well."

Heita Hoonoch whinnied and walked a few steps away. He could not flex the joint above his left front fetlock, and he limped as he walked. Gray Squirrel ran to him and felt his foreleg. There was no heat, only a hard swelling around the joint. It didn't seem to be painful. Somehow she knew this was how he had healed.

The girl looked into the horse's great dark eyes. Then he whinnied loudly and pushed at her with his nose.

"Come," he seemed to say.

Gray Squirrel climbed onto his back and they walked into the fog.

In a moment Heita Hoonoch quickened his pace, first to a trot and then a gallop. No longer did he limp—in fact, no longer did his hooves touch the ground. Like the dream she had had that last night on the island, they were flying.

Into the black night and over the forest they sailed. With her hands wrapped tightly in Heita Hoonoch's mane and her brown legs clinging against his ribs, she felt the wind rush by. Soon she could smell the salty, moist air of the ocean.

The horse descended slowly until they once again touched the earth. Gray Squirrel looked around. They were standing on top of a great sand dune. She recognized it, a huge mountain of sand formed by hundreds of years of shifting winds and storm surges. To the east was the vast ocean, and to the west she could see all the way across the Sound to the mainland.

She slid off Heita Hoonoch's back and gazed into the sea. No one who tried to paddle across that great water had ever come back. She wondered what mysteries lay on its other shore.

Suddenly Gray Squirrel saw something. The sea was calm and what she saw rocked gently beyond the surf. Then she remembered. It was the same ship they had seen in her last dream. Its white sails reflected the moonlight, resembling a sea gull floating and bobbing in the waves.

As Gray Squirrel stood next to Heita Hoonoch, fascinated by what she saw, another movement caught her eye. Men were rowing two smaller boats ashore. She watched as they landed and pulled the boats up on the beach. They were the white-skinned men from her other dream. Some had hair on their faces. They looked like strange beasts.

As the men came ashore, one carried a lance with a brightly colored banner. He plunged it into the sand and all the men kneeled in a circle around it.

Gray Squirrel cried out in her sleep, but only the gray owl who rested in a nearby pine tree heard her. He too called out sadly as darkness surrendered to the morning sky.

Chapter Seven

White Deer watched her granddaughter weaving the thin willow branches into a basket. Gray Squirrel's work was so fine and tight that the basket would carry water.

The child had not played games with the other children since the corn dance. Instead, whenever she was not working, the girl sat quietly or walked in the woods.

White Deer had taken her granddaughter to the elders to tell them about the vision of the men with pale skin and fiery hair. A council had been called. They believed Gray Squirrel's vision meant the white-skinned people would come again. They discussed how to prepare for the arrival of the strangers. The men remembered what their elders had told them many times around the council fires.

Wanchese spoke. "My father told me how the men were peaceful at first, and then they turned against our people. We were forced to drive them away, back across the ocean!"

"Yes, and in that struggle many of our people died, not only in the war but from the diseases they brought," remembered Okisco.

Manteo's turn came to speak. "Creator has instructed us to live in peace. I believe we should extend that peace offering to all men, whether they be red or white. I say we meet them in peace. We do not know what is in their hearts, not until we meet them for ourselves."

The council talked long into the night. Wanchese said they should be prepared for war should the white men return, but Great Hawk and Manteo said, "No, we should meet these strangers in peace."

They all agreed that they needed to be on watch. They would be alert and ready to protect their people.

The morning sun rose in the sky before the council was over. The members cast their votes and agreed to meet the white men in peace.

Gray Squirrel had never felt so tired. She came out of the lodge and walked past the edge of the village to the riverbank. A large sycamore tree spread its roots over the embankment. Thick green moss filled the space between its roots, making a soft cushion. Gray Squirrel sat down on the pillow of moss and leaned back against the tree's trunk, her arms resting on the thick roots that curled on both sides of her.

Then she closed her eyes and replayed the vision of the great boat and the strange men. She thought of Heita Hoonoch and a tear formed in the corner of her eye and slowly dropped onto her cheek.

She thought of how she had prayed for her brother's safety. Surely he was safe. Soon she would be able to carry him corn and breathe the warm sunny smell of him again. The thought of seeing her friend made the day's events a little easier to bear.

The girl prayed she would find Heita Hoonoch alive and well when she returned with her family to the islands. She slept in the arms of the sycamore tree until the dawn of the next day.

White Deer knew her granddaughter had journeyed from childhood into womanhood the night of the corn dance. Her first desire was to follow Gray Squirrel into the woods, but she didn't. She would have to leave her in the hands of Creator.

Still, she felt relief when Gray Squirrel joined her at breakfast, hungrily eating the little corn cakes.

"Grandmother, they voted for peace. I know that was the right decision. I believe Creator means for me to work for peace between our People and the strangers who will come. That will be a difficult task, won't it, Grandmother?" Gray Squirrel spoke solemnly.

"Yes, it will be hard. The hearts of mankind are often full of hate, but if that is what Creator intends for you to do He will give you the power to follow His will. And He has given you a helper. Heita Hoonoch was given to you for this reason. Listen, Granddaughter, listen to Creator. He will tell you what to do."

White Deer went back to her work of preparing for the trip to the islands. She always looked forward to the move, but this time she was apprehensive. She worried about what the return of the white men would mean to her people. She prayed silently that if they returned, it would be in peace.

Chapter Eight
Spring 1584

It was midday when the Paspatank finally reached the eastern shore of the Currituck Sound. They unpacked their dugout canoes and began the task of repairing and rebuilding their summer homes.

Gray Squirrel helped her family gather materials for their wickiup. They cut green poles from live oak trees for the frame, then tied bundles of grass into place for the thatching. By late afternoon the house was finished and White Deer was cooking their first meal of fresh fish.

As the sun set crimson behind the branches of the ancient trees, Gray Squirrel laid down to sleep. But as she lay on her bed her heart pounded so loudly it kept her awake. She listened to the night sounds: Frogs and crickets cheeped and an owl hooted in a nearby tree. Sleep finally came, but she did not hear the sound she most longed for, a whinny or snort from her brother, Heita Hoonoch.

When she woke, morning was only a hint. The ocean licked at the shore which was wrapped in a cool, damp mist. Where the sky met the sea, a blush of rose faded into silver-gray. Stars still twinkled and a sliver of moon was reflected in the water. Gray Squirrel crept out of the shelter and away from camp. She ran the rest of the way across the sand to the ridge of dunes that separated the Sound and Atlantic Ocean's shores.

She stood on top of the highest dune and searched the beach for the little horse. The grass and sea oats rattled in the breeze. The sand, sparkling like gold, stretched out as far as her eyes could see. Heita Hoonoch was nowhere to be seen.

Gray Squirrel called out his name and then whinnied to him. She waited. Her ears strained to hear him answer.

Turning around and around, she peered into every clump of trees on the Sound's shore and again, and searched the vast strip of beach. Still, she saw nothing. Sea gulls laughed at her as they swooped down to ride the waves. Gray Squirrel's heart filled with loneliness. She waited, then called again.

She had started to walk back down the dune and back to the camp when movement in the tall grass near the marsh caught her eye. She called once more. This time she heard a response, and fixed her gaze on the spot where she had seen the reeds moving.

Heita Hoonoch walked into the open and stopped, as if to be sure it was safe. She called again and ran down the sand dune as the horse trotted toward her.

She was not surprised to see the colt limping. It was exactly as in her dream. He stood patiently while she ran her hands down his legs until she found the hard swelling around the left fetlock. The injury had healed poorly, leaving the joint stiff.

Heita Hoonoch nuzzled at the girl's hand questioningly.

"Ah, are you looking for your corn? Did you think I would forget? Here it is. Eat!" Gray Squirrel held out the ear of dried corn. She giggled as he ate greedily.

"I believe you missed my gifts more than you missed me," the girl admonished her friend. "I can see winter was not kind to you. You are thin and your eyes are weary with struggle." She stroked his mane. "Our spirits were together many times in the dream world. There we saw many visions. The elders have listened and believe you are a messenger. We will be prepared to meet the white men in peace when they come. We will watch for them while our families reap the harvest of the sea."

Gray Squirrel longed to ride the colt, but, sensing his weakness, she knew that would be selfish. She would strengthen him with food and soon they would gallop along the beach together.

Chapter Nine

Gray Squirrel brought Heita Hoonoch corn every morning as she had the summer before. She encouraged him to walk along the beach with her. The healing waves caressed Heita Hoonoch's legs. They swam together in the Sound and the colt's muscles grew stronger and stronger.

Soon the horse was able to trot with ease. Gray Squirrel ran alongside him, her hair flowing behind her, catching glints of gold from the sun.

Each day Gray Squirrel scanned the horizon for the ship she had seen in her dream. The girl and the horse stood atop the highest sand dunes and watched.

Every afternoon Gray Squirrel helped her grandmother clean and dry the fish and pack them into baskets, mend nets, and weave new baskets. In the late afternoons, the girl and the colt watched for the ship while they explored the beach. By evening the air was filled with the aroma of chowder stewing in the cooking pots. Gray Squirrel went to bed every night in anticipation of a new day with her friend, her brother Heita Hoonoch.

This morning began like any other. The girl and her horse arrived at the water hole at the same time. Right away, Heita Hoonoch nuzzled Gray Squirrel's arm, looking for corn.

"Would you come, my brother, if it were not for this corn?" Gray Squirrel giggled as the colt gobbled the food greedily. She stroked his neck and fluffed his mane.

Suddenly her heart told her that the time was right. Today was the day. She leaned across the horse's back and scrambled on astride. Heita Hoonoch raised his head and turned his neck to look at her. Then he continued eating.

"What do you think? Are you strong enough to let me ride?"

Heita Hoonoch finished the corn and started to walk. Although the joint would always be somewhat stiff, it was not painful. He began to trot.

Gray Squirrel laughed out loud and held on tight to his mane. It was a bumpy ride.

"Stop! Stop! I am falling!" she cried.

It was too late. Gray Squirrel slid to the ground and rolled down the sand dune.

Heita Hoonoch watched her with a puzzled look in his eyes.

Still laughing, the girl stood up and walked back up the little hill, brushing sand off her bottom as she went. "Let's try that again."

This time she stayed on. She guided the horse to the ocean's edge by pulling on Heita Hoonoch's mane. When they reached the beach she squeezed her legs and shouted, "Faster, faster!"

Soon Heita Hoonoch was galloping. Water sprayed Gray Squirrel's face as she leaned over the horse's neck, fingers gripping his mane tightly. Sea gulls flew out of their path. Gray Squirrel shouted, "Yee-e-e-ya!" in sheer joy.

After a while Heita Hoonoch slowed to a trot. Gray Squirrel sat upright and looked across the water. The sea was calm today and white clouds dotted the blue sky. Beyond the breakers, porpoises were playing.

Gray Squirrel marveled at how far they had traveled in such a short time. She realized Heita Hoonoch's speed and stamina would make it possible to explore more of the island than ever before.

They crossed back over the dunes and to the woods that bordered the Sound. The shade of the oak trees and pines cooled the air. A trail made by deer and other wild animals led to the shore. The water was calm. The girl and her horse watched silently while a raccoon deftly scooped a small crab out of the water's edge. Tall egrets also stalked the shallows, catching small fish with their long beaks.

Gray Squirrel urged the colt to follow the beach

south. They rounded a small peninsula. The beach had washed away, leaving a steep bank. Heita Hoonoch had to pick his way carefully through the water and the maze of cypress knees. Gray Squirrel's heart felt full as she surveyed the beauty of the wetlands.

"Come, my brother, we must go. It is a long way back home and Grandmother will wonder where I am." Gray Squirrel turned the horse and they made their way back across the marsh until they reached the sand dunes again. They trotted along the ocean beach, where the sand was wet and packed hard by the waves.

☽

When Gray Squirrel entered the fishing village riding on Heita Hoonoch's back, it created great excitement.

"Grandmother! Look!" she called.

White Deer smiled at her granddaughter. "So, your friend has let you ride on his back," she exclaimed.

"Yes, see how strong he is. We traveled far south of here. I could see the island of the Roanoke."

White Deer looked worried. "You must have gone

a long way. Be careful."

"Oh, Grandmother! Heita Hoonoch can run like the wind. I am safe with him!"

"Even so, be careful."

"Yes, Grandmother," Gray Squirrel nodded in agreement.

By this time the other children had seen Gray Squirrel on Heita Hoonoch's back and were all begging to ride. Gray Squirrel slid off his back and helped a small girl clamber up. Then she walked alongside the horse. He seemed to take the task seriously, walking very slowly and staying right beside Gray Squirrel. The little girl was smiling, but held tight to the horse's mane as Gray Squirrel instructed her. The other children stood watching and giggling.

"Let me ride, too!"

"I bet I can ride that horse!"

All the children got a turn before Gray Squirrel turned him loose. Everyone laughed as he kicked up his heels and galloped out of sight.

Chapter Ten

Gray Squirrel had to remind herself of her grandmother's warning every day while she and Heita Hoonoch
explored parts of the island she had never seen before.
They galloped in the surf and climbed the sand dunes.
They took long walks in the forest, but did not roam as
far away as they had that first day.

The girl fashioned a rope by braiding strips of
rawhide. She took the sharp flint tool White Deer used
to make beads and drilled a hole in the center of two
pieces of antler she'd carved into a long triangle. Then
she ran the rope through the holes. The rope fit in Heita
Hoonoch's mouth, between the two cheek pieces, to form
a bit with enough rope on either side to reach around his
neck. Another length of rope ran from the cheek pieces,
over his head, and behind his ears. Now Gray Squirrel
could more easily guide him in whatever direction she
wanted him to go. She almost never fell off him now.
Even when he dodged the waves, quickly spinning away
from the big ones, she was able to sit, perfectly balanced,
on his back.

Every day they watched the horizon for any sign of the white men's ship, but saw nothing except the porpoises at play and the sea gulls bobbing in the waves. She began to wonder if her vision had only been a meaningless dream.

One hot midsummer day, Gray Squirrel was riding Heita Hoonoch along a tall ridge when he stopped and, with his ears pointed forward, stared out across the ocean. Gray Squirrel looked too. Her heart leaped and she clenched the reins so tightly her knuckles turned white. It was exactly like her dreams. The white sails made the boat look like a giant sea bird bobbing in the waves. It was a long way from shore, but she knew it was them.

Wheeling Heita Hoonoch around, she urged him into a gallop toward the camp.

By the time they burst into the village, Gray Squirrel could hardly speak. Her heart was pounding so hard she could hear it.

"They have come! They have come!" she shouted once she gained control of her voice.

Heita Hoonoch was so excited by her screams and her tight grip on the reins that he spun around in circles, as if making a war dance. His antics threatened White Deer's little melon patch.

"Calm down, child!" she commanded. "What is all this commotion about?"

"I saw them, I saw the boat. Just like the dream, it is the white men. They are coming!" Gray Squirrel finally eased her hold on the horse and bent over to give him an apologetic pat. He stopped spinning and stood quietly, although he also was panting for breath.

A crowd of curious women and children gathered around Gray Squirrel and her horse.

"Go signal to Black Feather," White Deer told one of the children standing nearby. "Calm down and tell me everything, Gray Squirrel." White Deer looked worried.

"Grandmother, Heita Hoonoch saw it first. Just like in my dreams, its great white sails looked like a big bird floating in the waves. The ship is far out in the water. I think it will land further down the beach. Oh, Grandmother! I am afraid."

"Don't be child. You have done well. We have been forewarned so we can prepare to meet these visitors in peace. Do not worry. Look! Black Feather is already coming." White Deer embraced her granddaughter and then turned to her husband. Gray Squirrel did not see the worried look they exchanged.

Chapter Eleven

For three days, the ship Gray Squirrel spotted stayed anchored offshore. Council drums sent the message throughout the islands, and all the native people knew it had arrived. Finally, the men decided they should make the first move and welcome the white men.

Black Feather caught a boatload of fish and rowed out to the ship. The white men were apprehensive at first but, being hungry, soon overcame their fear. Still, they did not come ashore.

That night Black Feather enthralled his listeners at the campfire with descriptions of the huge boat and its occupants. He wore clothes of strange materials given him by the white men.

"These men seem kind in spirit. They shared their meat and drink, which was not like anything I have tasted before. The belly of their ship is big enough for many men to stand in. They say they have sailed for two moons. They wish to explore our land."

Black Feather showed Great Hawk the gifts that the explorers had given him. There were axes and knives of metal and beads of many bright colors.

"The people call themselves 'English'. They wish to trade more of these things for furs and food. They want to meet us in peace."

Great Hawk didn't speak for a long time. Then he stood. "We have been forewarned of these events by Creator through the dreams of this child. It is His will that we welcome these new people in peace. Their gifts are good. These tools are sharp and much better than the ones we make from stone. Let us all go tomorrow and meet these men. We will call a council with them and our brothers in the neighboring tribes."

The next day the men, about forty in all, paddled their boats out to the white men's ship. The People provided the English with food and shelter and traded furs for the marvelous tools and fancy things brought from the other side of the ocean. Gray Squirrel often rode Heita Hoonoch to the place where the ship was anchored offshore and watched.

For two months, the Englishmen explored the land and traded with the people they met in their travels. Then the time came for them to return to their homeland. They invited some of the tribal elders to sail with them, and Manteo and Wanchese agreed to go.

Gray Squirrel felt much fear in her heart for these two leaders. None of her people who tried to navigate that great water had ever come back. Although she was afraid, a small part of her was curious to know what lay beyond the horizon.

☽

One year later, the English returned with Wanchese, Manteo, and about one hundred men. The white men explored further inland and continued trading with the people they met.

Before long, conflict developed. The English became involved in war between two inland tribes. News of the unrest spread to all of the People. There seemed little hope of achieving peace between the native tribes and the Englishmen.

By this time the Paspatank had returned to their village; the fishing was done. The only thing that gave Gray Squirrel happiness in this difficult time was that Heita Hoonoch was strong enough to come with her, swimming alongside her canoe as she and her family paddled across the shallow Currituck Sound.

There were new places to explore, and often she went with her grandfather to hunt. Heita Hoonoch made it possible to travel longer distances in search of game, and he could carry a large deer carcass on his back, making it faster and easier to bring the meat back to the village.

Meanwhile, in spite of Manteo and Great Hawk's protests, war broke out between the Indians and the white visitors, and many men were killed. The surviving Englishmen retreated and sailed back to their homeland.

The fighting made Gray Squirrel's spirit dark with sadness. When she was not working, she and Heita Hoonoch took long rides deep into the forest. She found solace in his companionship, but the joy had escaped her spirit. She had failed to do what Creator had asked of her.

Chapter Twelve

1587

It had been three years since the English fled the barrier islands. Peace had returned to the land, and the Paspatank once again followed their traditional migration across the Currituck to harvest the sea's gift of food for their people.

Gray Squirrel rode Heita Hoonoch through the dunes and the maritime woods, but her heart was not as full of adventure as in the summers past.

She was a young woman of twelve summers now. She spent most of the day helping her grandmother with the fish, mending nets and making baskets. She no longer had dreams of flying through the night sky with the bay colt.

The horse made the work easier. Often when the nets were heavy with fish, Gray Squirrel fastened a rope around Heita Hoonoch's neck, then ran it through the net. The horse could do the work of several men, pulling in the net with ease.

One sunny July morning, Gray Squirrel finished

her work earlier than usual. On the way to meet Heita Hoonoch, she picked flowers and wove them into her long black hair. It was a mild day, and the sea breezes chased away the heat.

She discovered Heita Hoonoch grazing at the bottom of the dunes. He whinnied and then continued grazing, content to let her come to him. She greeted him affectionately and offered him some corn.

Gray Squirrel didn't notice the drums at first, but as they became more urgent she stopped to listen. The drums were signaling the arrival of strangers.

"Let us go see who is coming," she said as she slipped the bridle over his head.

Gray Squirrel was curious to see who had come to the islands. The sound of the drums came from the south, from the Hatteras most likely. She thought they probably signaled the arrival of people from one of the western villages coming to trade or fish. The drums did not sound an alarm, so she did not consider danger.

As Heita Hoonoch galloped in the surf and then across the dunes, the red and gold flowers in Gray Squirrel's hair caught the sunlight.

She saw the familiar white sails miles before she reached her destination. They were back. Her heart was hard; she wished they would stay on the other side of the ocean. She slowed Heita Hoonoch to a walk. Only trouble followed these strangers, bearers of sickness and war.

She turned to go back, not wanting to lay her eyes upon the men again. But Heita Hoonoch stopped, and Gray Squirrel saw that the ship was sailing back out to sea. Then she saw a group of people standing on the beach.

"What is this? The boat is leaving some behind. Look! They have brought women and children!" Gray Squirrel was astonished. "Surely they would not have brought their families if they had come to make war on us."

Gray Squirrel guided her mount down the back side of the dunes and into the shelter of the moss-covered trees. "I want to get a better look. Oh, there is Manteo talking with them."

Just then she heard a loud cry from some of the men on shore, who raised their fists in anger at the ship as it sailed away.

Gray Squirrel cued Heita Hoonoch to walk closer to the scene. She noticed a mother with her arms around a young boy. Tears were streaming down the woman's face.

Gray Squirrel rode her horse out of the trees and approached them. Her heart was suddenly full of compassion for this woman and her child.

"My name is Gray Squirrel," she introduced herself to the mother and son. She had learned how to speak English from the explorers who had come before. "What has happened?"

"They have left us," the woman said flatly. "Now we will surely perish in this wilderness."

Gray Squirrel felt the fear in the woman's voice and saw the little boy tremble. She smiled at him. "Can he ride?" she asked his mother, motioning to the boy and then to the space behind her on Heita Hoonoch's back.

The woman's eyes focused on the Indian girl and her horse. She looked horrified. "No!" she cried. "Get away from my boy, you savage!"

Gray Squirrel could read the disgust and fear in the woman's voice. She turned to go.

"Please, Mama! I want to ride! Please!" the little boy begged.

Gray Squirrel stopped and looked back. "I mean you no harm," she said. She took the flowers from her hair and held them out to the woman.

The Englishwoman saw the compassion in Gray Squirrel's eyes and relented. She nodded reluctantly, and Gray Squirrel reached down to help the boy onto Heita Hoonoch's back.

"What is your name?" she asked him.

"William," the boy answered. "What is yours?"

"My name is Gray Squirrel."

"You have a pretty horse. I had to leave my pony at home," the boy said. "What is his name?"

"Heita Hoonoch—Moon Wind in your language. He is my brother. He will take us anywhere I ask." Gray Squirrel reined the horse around and they started up the beach.

They rode down the beach and across a ridge of sand dunes. From the top they could see all the way to the mainland. Gray Squirrel pointed out the direction of her family's fishing camp. They galloped back along the beach where they had left the stranded families.

Gray Squirrel joined her neighbors in helping William's family and the others build lean-to shelters. Then they built a cooking fire and grilled some fish.

After everyone had eaten, Gray Squirrel turned to William. "I have to return to my camp before my grandmother worries," she told him, "but I will tell her that all of you are here. Tomorrow I will come back, and we will ride some more," Gray Squirrel promised.

Chapter Thirteen

The English colonists, before being abandoned by their captain, had originally planned to sail up the coast to the Chesapeake Bay area. John White's intention was to stop at Hatteras only long enough to look for a group of men who stayed behind on the last trip. Stranded, they decided to build houses on a large island which was situated between the Outer Banks and the mainland. It was called Roanoke. Gray Squirrel convinced her people to help the white men build houses.

White Deer and her granddaughter showed the women how to plant gardens and to use healing herbs. They taught them to bury a fish with each hill of corn and beans. The fish would give the seeds strength so the plants would bear more food and the corn stalks would act as a support for the bean vines. William's mother shared seeds that she had brought from her homeland with White Deer.

The warm sun and gentle rains brought the seeds to life and the English gardens flourished. So did the friendship between the white colonists and the Indian families.

When the tide was low, Gray Squirrel and Heita Hoonoch could swim to Roanoke Island. A sandbar midway between the two shores gave them a place to stop and rest. She visited William often and their friendship grew strong. Gray Squirrel was very happy. She was especially happy that her people were able to forgive the past misdeeds of these strangers' countrymen.

The summer passed swiftly and the time came for the Paspatank to return to their village on the mainland.

"We will come back in the spring," Gray Squirrel promised William.

"I will be lonely without you and Heita Hoonoch to play with. Who will take me exploring while you are gone?" William bent over and drew circles in the sand with a stick. He was a little embarrassed to show such emotion to a girl.

"We have today. Come, we will have a great adventure! Swim with me back to my camp. We will ride Heita Hoonoch to the top of the sand mountain.

You will be able to see all the way to the mainland and the great ocean. To the north and south the beach stretches like a long ribbon rippling in a breeze." Gray Squirrel's black eyes danced with excitement.

"You are crazy. I can't swim across the Sound!" William protested, but he knew Gray Squirrel and her pony swam across often. He'd have to meet her challenge.

"Come, we must go now, while the tide is out. We can touch the bottom most of the way. The only hard part is the channel, where the water runs deep and fast. You can do it!" Gray Squirrel was already tugging at William's shirtsleeve.

William hopped up on Heita Hoonoch's back behind Gray Squirrel. They rode out of the palisade gate and down the trail which led to the sandy beach. Gray Squirrel guided her pony to a point that reached out into the Sound.

Heita Hoonoch did not hesitate to walk out into the water.

"We will get off now and let him swim beside us. If you get tired just grab onto his mane," Gray Squirrel instructed.

"But it is so far!"

"Don't worry. We can do it! See, there is the sandbar I told you about. You can see it from here. The channel is on the other side of it."

And so the threesome waded out and then began to swim. William got tired before they were midway between the beach and the sandbar. He did as his friend had instructed and grabbed hold of the colt's mane, floating along as the strong little horse swam with ease. When he had rested he let go and swam some more. He noticed that Gray Squirrel did not get tired. She swam with graceful, long strokes, hardly making so much as a ripple in the water. He was ashamed for being weaker than a girl.

Finally they reached the sandbar. William fell spread-eagled on the sand. He was breathing hard.

"We will rest here awhile," said Gray Squirrel, patting Heita Hoonoch's neck. "When we get to the other side, we will eat the cornbread and dried fish I left in a special hiding place. We will eat before we explore."

William noticed that neither Gray Squirrel nor her pony seemed tired. He felt the sun hot on his face. It was early in the day; by noon it would really be hot.

"I'm fine now. Are you ready?" he asked bravely.

"Are you sure? Have you rested enough?" Gray Squirrel looked at William as if trying to judge whether she thought they should go on.

"Yes, I am ready!" William stood up to prove he was well rested.

"Do you see where the water is a darker blue? That is the channel. It will pull us south a ways, but that is okay. Don't let it scare you and don't fight it. It will actually carry us closer to land. Another point, like the one where we started, will be only a short distance from where the current will take us. Then we must swim our strongest. And we will have made it!"

William nodded and the three entered the sound on the other side of the sandbar. For a long way out they could still touch the sandy bottom with their toes. Heita Hoonoch swam between the girl and the boy.

Soon William could see they were close to the deep blue water, the channel. He reached for Heita

Hoonoch's mane, but missed. The colt was out of reach. William felt a stab of panic as he felt the water pull at him. It was cold. He began to swim frantically, flailing his arms and splashing at the waves.

"Don't!" shouted Gray Squirrel. "Don't be afraid. Relax and be with its spirit. The current will bring you over."

William heard his friend and her words encouraged him. He reached out to the colt and caught hold of his tail. That was enough to give him a chance to come up for air. He could see the sandy point. It was not far.

"Now, William, swim toward the point!"

William made one last heroic effort. They were free of the current and soon he felt the bottom again with his toes.

"We made it!" he shouted. "Now I am really tired." William dropped onto the warm sand. "You do this all the time? I can't believe you haven't drowned."

"It is because Heita Hoonoch and I have been swimming a lot. Don't worry, I will take you back in a canoe." Gray Squirrel smiled at her friend. "You did very well. You only need to practice more to make yourself stronger. And you must listen to the spirit of the water and let it lead you. Never fight it, it is too strong and you cannot win."

"Where is that lunch you told me you have hidden? I am starving!" William sat up and looked around as if he might find the food close at hand.

"Ah, we will have to go a little ways. It is in a tree." Gray Squirrel got on the colt's back and waited for William to do the same.

Moss dripped from the branches of a twisted, old oak tree. Gray Squirrel guided Heita Hoonoch through the curtain of moss to the trunk and reached into the fork where the tree split into two thick limbs. She handed William the lunch she had hidden. They ate under the shade of the tree while Heita Hoonoch grazed nearby. A breeze chased away the heat of the noonday sun.

Gray Squirrel and her two best friends, an English boy and a dark bay horse, played along the Sound's shore for a while. Thoughts of separation were far from their minds. A blue heron stalked small fish in the reeds at the water's edge while red winged blackbirds darted in and out of the sea oats.

"Enough rest," Gray Squirrel announced eventually. "Come, William. We will ride to the top of the great sand mountain, look for porpoises, and see the eagle fly toward the mainland. Perhaps you will see all the way across the ocean to your homeland." Gray Squirrel was already seated on her pony's back. She held her hand out to William, who took it and vaulted up behind her.

Heita Hoonoch took off at a trot and William held tight to his friend's waist. Soon the pony moved into an easy gallop. They followed a trail through the old oak trees. Gray moss hung from the branches and wisped at the children's faces as the horse carried them.

The trail opened out into a stretch of sand and low dunes. The colt was sweating. Foam had formed on his chest and between his hind legs. Gray Squirrel reined him to a stop. "Rest, my brother. It is hot. We can walk awhile."

The two riders dismounted and walked alongside the horse for a mile or so. Clouds had formed in the sky and soon showered the three with a light rain. It was cool and refreshing. Gray Squirrel danced in circles with her arms outstretched. She held her head back to catch the raindrops in her open mouth. Her black hair swung out behind her like a bird's wings in flight. William thought for a moment that she looked beautiful; she seemed to fit right in with the sea and sky and the forest. She was like the deer and the eagle, part of God's creation. She knew how to be one with nature.

They could see the huge sand dune up ahead, looming above the landscape like the chest of some sleeping monster. As they approached the base William could see little ripples formed by the shifting, windswept sand. Here the sand was packed hard and walking became much easier. The wind was stronger since the shower, and sand blew across the surface. It made a veil, obscuring the outline of the ridge.

"Hop up," Gray Squirrel told her friend. "Get ready for a ride!"

William was settled on Heita Hoonoch's back and had his arms wrapped tightly around his friend's waist. Gray Squirrel leaned forward and squealed into the colt's ear. Instantly his hooves dug into the deep sand and he took off up the side of the mammoth sand dune at a full gallop.

William shouted, "Whoa!" but neither the girl or the horse heard him, so he just hung on for dear life. When they reached the top, Gray Squirrel reined her pony to a stop.

William was about to reprimand his friend for scaring the daylights out of him, but as soon as he looked around at the view from the top of the sand dune he was speechless. The three friends stood silently and gazed in all directions. It seemed endless. The ocean and sandy beach to the east stretched out as far as they could see. Then William looked to his left. He saw the Croatan and Roanoke Sounds, and Roanoke Island like a big green egg in the middle.

They stood that way in silence for a long time. The wind blew sand around their legs, swirling upward until it stung their faces. Heita Hoonoch stood beside them, his head held high, eyes dark and bright. His mane and tail sailed in the wind. His flanks were still wet from the rain, and the droplets of water caught glints of sunlight and sparkled like tiny diamonds.

Gray Squirrel pointed toward the ocean. "Porpoises! Look, look. There they are just beyond the breakers."

William looked and giggled in delight. A large group of twenty or more porpoises were rolling with the waves. They arched up out of the water and back under over and over again, looking like a single body.

"We saw a whale on our journey from England," said William. His voice seemed as far away as the country he mentioned.

"Do you miss it?" asked the girl.

"I will miss it even more when you leave. You are lucky to be able to go home. I don't believe I will ever see my homeland again," William answered.

"We never know what the future holds for us. Perhaps you are right, but the English have made the voyage from my land to yours many times already. I believe you will have an opportunity to go back one day," Gray Squirrel reassured him.

"Yes, you are right. I thank you for making my new home less lonely. You are a good friend, Gray

Squirrel. I know the winter will seem very long when you leave. I will miss you and Heita Hoonoch and the fun we've had." William didn't look at Gray Squirrel when he spoke. Instead, he patted the colt on the neck and continued to watch the porpoises playing. He didn't want his friend to see the tears that were welling up in his eyes.

"Yonder is my homeland." Gray Squirrel pointed to the north and west. "You cannot see it, it is so far away. We will cross the Currituck and follow a trail a long distance."

William wondered at the vastness of what lay beyond his vision. It was a "goodly land" just as their expedition's leader, John White, had promised him and his mother.

Chapter Fourteen

The winter was a hard one for the colonists. Food became scarce and the people were discontented. Many of the Indians had retreated from the coast. There were disputes again between them and the white men. The Indians grew tired of hunting and fishing for the colonists, who seemed either too lazy or too stupid to learn to take care of themselves. The white men grew impatient with the 'share and share alike' lifestyle of the People. They accused some of the braves of stealing, and wanted to punish them. These disputes became more and more serious.

Gray Squirrel heard rumors of the strained tensions between the English and the coastal tribes. She heard too of the sickness which had plagued many of the coastal villages. Many of the People had died of diseases that the medicine chiefs could not heal. Gray Squirrel prayed to Creator for peace and healing.

That winter her dreams were unfruitful. She was in despair. Then one night she dreamed that she and Heita Hoonoch were following a strange path, deep into the swamp. They traveled all night long until the trail opened into a clearing. There she saw a lake with a sandy beach. She saw smoke rising from cooking fires and then she saw a village.

Gray Squirrel woke up from the dream confused. Where was this trail and whose village was that beside the lake?

⏾

By the time she returned to the islands and the Paspatank's summer fishing camp, the unrest between the English and some of the coastal tribes was close to the breaking point.

White Deer warned Gray Squirrel not to go to Roanoke Island to visit William.

"Surely the colonists will not harm us," Gray Squirrel implored. "I promised William I would come back. He is my friend!"

The grandmother was sad to see the hurt in Gray Squirrel's eyes, but she was firm. Her granddaughter must stay near the camp.

Gray Squirrel obeyed her grandmother and confined her rides with Heita Hoonoch to the north beaches, close to the Paspatank camp.

She worried as she heard more stories of arguments between the men of neighboring tribes and the English. It seemed that as the summer became hotter, so did the tempers of the two sides.

Chapter Fifteen
March 1589

Gray Squirrel listened to Wanchese's voice and shivered at the rage in his words. A council had been called, and Wanchese inflamed the spirits of the elders over the afternoon's unjust events.

She knew he was right to be angry. She knew because she saw the man named Thomas give the silver cup to a Croatan brave. Thomas gave it to him in trade for a stone that was the color of the sun. Gold.

The Croatan had been wearing the stone around his neck since the spring corn festival. That was where he had traded with a Cherokee boy who wanted his necklace of shell beads.

When the Englishmen found the Croatan with the cup, they accused him of stealing it. In the course of the argument, one of the white men shot and killed the Croatan brave.

Wanchese declared war on all of the settlers. "They have brought disease and trouble to our people. We should never have allowed them back on this land.

They are full of deceit. They have taken our help and repaid us with treachery."

The young braves shouted and shook their weapons. Gray Squirrel knew there would be a war. She had to warn her friends. William and his family would be in danger.

She listened as Wanchese told the men to meet him at dawn to launch their canoes. They would cross the water and attack Fort Raleigh. They would rid the islands of the white people once and for all.

Gray Squirrel found Heita Hoonoch grazing near the water hole. She had never disobeyed her grandmother before, but if she didn't warn her friends they would all die. She slipped the bridle over the horse's head; then she hopped onto his back.

The moonlight made it easy to see their way as they walked quietly to the other side of the sand dunes. There the girl urged him into a gallop. The soft sand muffled the sound of his hoofbeats. They traveled south and then crossed back over the dunes to the Sound's shore.

The full moon beamed a silver path across the

calm water, as if leading them to the other side. Gray Squirrel urged the horse into the water. He walked past the treeline until he was chest-deep, and then he began swimming. Gray Squirrel slid off his back and held onto his mane with one hand while she swam alongside him. Only his head was above water.

They swam on and on, the moon still lighting their path. The tide was in, making the current run swiftly. Gray Squirrel shut the fear out of her heart. She refused to think of the alligators that made their home on the swampy shoreline or the beasts that lived in the water.

When they were halfway across the channel, Gray Squirrel could feel the current pull at them. It was pulling them further south; they had to swim harder, or they would wash out to the greater vast part of the Croatan Sound and there would be no turning back.

"Don't give up, my brother," she urged. "Follow the path of the moon. Remember the moon is your strength. We must reach the colony before Wanchese launches the canoes and brings his war party."

Heita Hoonoch was slowing. He faltered and

his head disappeared under the water.

"No! Don't stop!" Gray Squirrel reached for his mane to pull him up, but felt nothing. Heita Hoonoch had disappeared into the black depths.

A cloud covered the moon and the silver path vanished into the night. Gray Squirrel tried hard to push away her fear, but it rose up in her throat and nearly choked her. She looked around for the trees on the shoreline, but the darkness made it impossible to see which way to go.

"Heita Hoonoch!" she called, but only an owl, hooting in the distance, replied.

Gray Squirrel treaded water and listened. The owl hooted again, and Gray Squirrel swam toward the sound. She knew that the owl lived in the trees, and following his call would take her toward land.

A light breeze rippled the water's surface and the cloud broke away from the moon. The moon's blue-white light again marked a path across the water.

Gray Squirrel could see the trees etched against the sky. The shore was near, but where was Heita Hoonoch?

When Gray Squirrel reached the sandy beach of Roanoke Island, she had no strength left and could only lie in the sand, with the water still lapping over her legs. She fell asleep. She did not notice the dark figure standing under the moss-laden cypress trees.

The figure walked out of the shadows and approached cautiously. Its sides heaved as it breathed heavily.

Standing next to Gray Squirrel's body, Heita Hoonoch pawed at the sand. Then he nudged at her shoulder with his muzzle. Still, Gray Squirrel did not move. The horse raised his head and let out a loud whinny.

Somewhere in Gray Squirrel's unconscious mind, she stood on top of the tallest sand dune and searched the beach for her friend and brother. She heard him whinny a greeting as he galloped to her, but just as he reached her side he disappeared and her mind sunk back into darkness.

Gray Squirrel struggled in her dream world. They were outside the English palisade. Just beyond was a thicket of pines and oaks dripping with gray moss. Heita Hoonoch stood before her on a trail. She rose up and followed him. She didn't recognize this place. Thick reeds and vines made it look impossible to penetrate. But with each step she took it seemed to open up before them.

"Where are we going?" she questioned.

Heita Hoonoch stopped until she stood beside him. He turned his head and looked into her eyes. There was an urgency in his gaze, and she knew they must keep going. He waited for her to climb on his back, and then he continued down the dense path.

The trail grew darker and darker. The two friends were swallowed up by the forest, and Gray Squirrel struggled to come out of the dream because she was afraid.

Chapter Sixteen

Heita Hoonoch sniffed at the girl's body lying face down in the sand. He nudged her hand. She didn't move.

The moon was sinking below the horizon, leaving the sky black before dawn. The horse whinnied, softly first, then emphatically, so that his voice echoed across the water. Gray Squirrel let go of the dream spirit. She moaned and tried to move, but she was so tired.

Finally she found the strength to turn over and open her eyes. Heita Hoonoch blew his breath softly across her face.

"Oh no, it is nearly dawn," she breathed. "We still have to reach the fort and warn them."

Gray Squirrel slowly sat up. She reached for her friend's mane and twisted it in her hand. Heita Hoonoch lifted his head and pulled the girl to her feet. With great effort, she climbed onto his back.

"Please, my brother. We cannot quit now. A little further. That way through the woods."

She knew Wanchese and his men would now be launching their canoes. It would not be long before they reached this shore. Once again she urged the horse into a gallop. He ran until she pulled him to a stop at the fort's gate.

"Who goes there!" called out a guard.

"It is Gray Squirrel. Hurry, I have come to warn you of danger."

The guard, recognizing her voice, let her in. "What is wrong?" he questioned.

"Wanchese has gathered many warriors. They are coming now, across the Sound. They are very angry. A Croatan was shot by one of your men. They intend to kill all of the people in the colony. Heita Hoonoch has given me his strength and speed so I can warn you. Gather your people now!"

"Sound the alarm!" shouted the guard.

Quickly the men, women, and children assembled in the courtyard.

"Into your boats," Gray Squirrel pleaded. "I have been shown a trail which will lead you to safety, but first we must reach the mainland. Hurry! Wanchese and his war party are on their way. They will be here soon."

The women were tying bundles of their belongings into blankets, grabbing what seemed most important.

"Come, you haven't time," Gray Squirrel urged them.

"Wait, we are to leave a message," said William. "I'll carve it on this tree where Mr. White will be sure to see it when he returns. I will write CROATAN ATTACK."

"No, we haven't time, William," Gray Squirrel insisted. She pulled at William's arm, interrupting him before he could finish carving the message. 'CROATAN' was as far as he got before his friend urgently pulled him to the waiting boats. Gray Squirrel sat in one of the boats, while her faithful pony once again plunged into the water and swam alongside.

By the time the group pulled their boats onto the beach of the mainland, they could see pillars of smoke rising from the island. "Oh dear, they are burning the fort," exclaimed William's mother. "Dear Gray Squirrel, you have surely saved us all from perishing!" William's mother was crying now.

"Come, follow me." Gray Squirrel's heart was

racing. She remembered the trail from her dreams; she recognized everything surrounding her. That was the message in her dreams. Creator had shown her a way to protect the English colony.

"This way—there is a trail," Gray Squirrel shouted as she leaped onto Heita Hoonoch's back. She remembered every moss-drenched tree and every twist and turn through the thick underbrush. She guided Heita Hoonoch west through the swamp and the people followed. No one made a sound. It was as if she had followed the trail a thousand times.

Deeper into the forest, the woods were so thick with vines that the sun's light could hardly break through. The trail rose above the murky black water of the swamp, and the tall reeds seemed to open up and beckon the people to follow.

☽

It was the middle of the next day before they reached the village of the Lake People.

"They are here, they are here!" shouted a crowd of children greeting them as the trail opened into a clearing. It was exactly as Gray Squirrel had dreamed—a wide sandy beach at the edge of a lake. A dozen wickiups dotted the landscape.

Gray Squirrel smelled food. The group had eaten nothing but some berries they picked along the trail, and everyone was hungry.

It was obvious that the People were expecting visitors. The English were welcomed warmly and a feast was prepared for them.

After they had eaten and were resting around the cooking fire, Gray Squirrel asked the elders, "How did you know we were coming?"

The chief elder answered her, "I was told in a dream. I dreamed I was hunting and a great bear appeared and spoke to me. He told me to prepare a feast to welcome a people new to this land. He told me a young girl riding a dark horse would be leading a people whose skin is as pale as the moon, and we should make them our people. So when I woke I told my village to prepare for your arrival."

Gray Squirrel nodded in understanding. By the time
the sun set, she had fallen asleep. Heita Hoonoch grazed
among the reeds close by. Tomorrow they would go
home.

Epilogue

War with Spain delayed John White's return to his colony. When he returned to Roanoke Island in August 1590 he found the place where he had left the colony empty, the houses torn down and ground scattered with various items too heavy to transport on foot. On a tree near the shore the letters CRO were carved and on another tree nearer the fort was written CROATOAN. Seeing no cross which would have indicated distress, he assumed the colonists had moved further south to live near the Croatans, near Hatteras. Bad weather prevented further investigation, and White returned to England believing the colonists had survived. He died, never able to return to the family he left behind in the New World. The lost colony has remained a mystery.

☽

In 1956 the West Virginia Pulp and Paper Co. was digging canals and building logging roads for their operation in the area of Buffalo City near East Lake in

Dare County, about thirty miles inland from Roanoke Island. A man dug into a mound with his bulldozer and unearthed Indian artifacts, along with some coffins. The coffins had been fashioned by lashing two dugout canoes together. On the outside, crosses and other Christian symbols had been carved.

The man was instructed to cover the artifacts back up. The area later became a bombing range, so the find was never studied and the evidence that might have unlocked the mystery was forever destroyed.

Some Historical Notes

While *Pale as the Moon* is a fictional story and the characters are products of the imagination, the book does reflect a historical time and place. Wild ponies, descendants of the horses brought to the New World in the early sixteenth century, still roam the Outer Banks.

In 1524, Giovanni da Verrazano explored the area north of Kitty Hawk. Ships' records of Verrazano and other Spanish explorers show they brought horses, swine and cattle with them.

Luis Vazquez de Ayllon tried to establish a colony on the Carolina coast in 1526. He brought 500 men, women, children and slaves, and 90 horses.

The Spanish did not deal fairly with the Native People, and wars ensued. Defeated, the Spaniards sailed down the coast to Florida. They left their horses behind.

We can only guess how the horses' arrival altered the culture of the Native People of America. At first, horses might have seemed like fearsome animals—but it wouldn't have taken long for the Indians to realize that these large creatures were gentle beasts, willing to share their strength and stamina.

The Spaniards' horses, which were from the deserts of Arabia, adapted easily to the sandy beaches of their new home. When the English arrived 50 years later, they found that the Native People had adopted some of the horses as pets, feeding and taking care of them. They also used some of the horses as beasts of burden. The remaining horses roamed freely, as they still do today.

Unfortunately, the Native Americans, who comprised at least 30 tribes along the Carolina coast, did not survive the coming of the Europeans as well as did the horses. Many died from diseases such as small pox and measles. They had no immunity against the illnesses introduced to the New World by the white invaders. The settlers soon overpowered the Indians, and the tribes dwindled in number as their members were driven from their homes.

We do not know very much about the people who lived in America before the explorers and colonists came. The newcomers were more interested in finding gold and other valuable resources than they were in the people they encountered. The writings and drawings of John White are the best records we have. Two other English explorers who also wrote about the Indians were Thomas Harriot and John Lawson.

You can learn more about wild ponies, Native Americans and the early exploration of the upper coastal region of North Carolina by visiting your local library or contacting the following:

Currituck Beach Lighthouse
Corolla, NC 27927
(252) 453-8152

Fort Raleigh National Historic Site
Rt. 1, Box 675, Manteo, NC 27954
(252) 473-5773

> See the outdoor drama, *The Lost Colony*, at the Waterside Theatre, Fort Raleigh National Historic Site (early June - late August).
> (252) 473-3414

Frisco Native American Museum

PO Box 399, Frisco, NC 27936

(252) 995-4440

Wolf Creek Indian Village and Museum

Rt. 1 Box 1530, Bastian, VA 24314

(540) 688-3438

North Carolina Dept. of Administration, NC
Commission of Indian Affairs

217 Jones Street, Raleigh, NC 27603-1336

(919) 733-5998

Corolla Wild Horse Fund of Outer Banks
Conservationists, Inc.

PO Box 970, Manteo, NC 27954

Outer Banks Lighthouse Society

PO Box 305, Kill Devil Hills, NC 27948

(252) 441-9928

Elizabeth II State Historic Site
PO Box 155, Manteo, NC 27954
(252) 473-1144

All of the books in the bibliography can be found at your local library, or at the gift shops and bookstores of most Outer Banks communities.

Bibliography

Barefoot, Daniel W. *Touring the Backroads of North Carolina's Upper Coast*. Winston-Salem: John F. Blair Publisher, 1995

Harriot, Thomas. *A Briefe and True Report of the New Found Land of Virginia*. New York: Dover Publications, Inc., 1992

Lawson, John. *A New Voyage to Carolina*. Edited by Hugh Ralmage Lefler. Chapel Hill: The University of North Carolina Press, 1967

Rights, Douglas L. *The American Indian in North Carolina*. 2nd edition. *Winston-Salem: John F. Blair, 1957*

Study Guide

A stranded colt and a young Native American girl develop a bond as they strive to survive in the harsh conditions of Coastal Carolina in the sixteenth century. Gray Squirrel is forewarned, through a series of dreams, of the arrival of a strange people with skin as pale as the moon. Empowered by the speed and stamina of the horse, the girl plays a major role in the protection of an abandoned English colony. Shrouded in mystery to this day, the demise of John White's colony remains the secret of Heita Hoonoch and Gray Squirrel.

Study Questions:

Q1. In the first two chapters, what did you learn about the coast of North Carolina in the 16th century?

Q2. Is coastal North Carolina different today than it was 500 years ago?

Q3. Why do you think Gray Squirrel and Heita Hoonoch had such a special bond?

Q4. What character qualities did Gray Squirrel have that made Heita Hoonoch finally trust her?

Q5. How did the Paspatank people study history?

Q6. What was the purpose of the corn festival?

Q7. What happened to Heita Hoonoch in the winter when Gray Squirrel had to leave without him?

Q8. Why did the Paspatank visit the Outer Banks in the summer?

Q9. How did the elders feel when Gray Squirrel told them about her dreams?

Q10. What was the relationship like between the English and Indians in the beginning? Did it change? Why?

Q11. What did William's mother think about Gray Squirrel when they first met?

Q12. Did she change her mind? Why?

Study Question Answers:

A1. The weather was sometimes stormy. Some of the plants that grew there were sea oats, trees, and shrubs. There were a lot of mosquitoes in summer. It got very hot in summer, but breezes from the ocean made it cooler. There were forests and sand dunes.

A2. Yes. 500 years ago the islands were covered with forests. Most of the forests are gone now because the early settlers cut down most of the trees to build ships and houses. The cedar trees and cypress were valued for shipbuilding. Now many people live on the Outer Banks, and there are hotels, condos and shopping centers instead of woods.

A3. They were both orphans.

A4. Patience, kindness, generosity.

A5. By telling stories passed down from generation to generation.

A6. It was a time of giving thanks to Creator for the past harvest and to ask His blessing for the spring planting. The People forgave any wrongs done them, and it was also a chance to visit and trade with friends and neighbors.

A7. He slipped on ice and hurt his leg. Food was hard to find and he got very thin.

A8. To fish and preserve the fish for the winter. They dried the fish and packed them in baskets to carry home to their village.

A9. They were worried because they recalled when the Spanish explorers had visited their land. Many of their children were kidnapped and there was war between the Spanish and Native People. Many people died from war and disease. They believed her dream meant the white-skinned people would come again.

The elders argued about how to prepare for the arrival of these strangers. They decided to meet them in peace, but to be careful.

A10. The Native People met the English in peace and helped them gather food and build their homes. But they did not understand each other's culture and they began to distrust each other. Greed and distrust led to disagreements and war.

A11. That Gray Squirrel was a savage. William's mother was afraid of her.

A12. Yes. She realized Gray Squirrel was just a little girl who was kind and only wanted to be a friend. Gray Squirrel gave the mother flowers and let William ride Heita Hoonoch.

Discussion Questions:

Q. What do you think happened to the Lost Colony?

Q. Do you think the Paspatank children were alike or different from children today? Why?

Q. How do you think the English children felt about coming to the New World?

Q. Some people say the reason we study history is to learn things about ourselves. Have you learned anything about yourself while studying sixteenth-century North Carolina?

Dates to Remember:

1540 - De Soto visited the coastal regions of what is now North Carolina, the first of a series of Spanish explorations of the area. These explorers treated the Native People badly and were driven back to Florida. They left horses and livestock behind.

1584 - Sir Walter Raleigh's first exploration of the North Carolina coast. Returned two months later and gave a glowing report of the land.

1585 - Raleigh sent a colony to America under Sir Richard Grenville. Ralph Lane was chosen as the colony's governor. The 108 male colonists, who included future Roanoke Island governor John White, spent more time trying to find gold and other riches than trying to establish the colony. They failed and returned to England with Sir Francis Drake.

1587 - In April, Raleigh sent a second colony, with John White as its governor. This colony consisted of

150 men, women and children. They meant to settle in the Chesapeake Bay area, but they stopped at Roanoke to find 15 men left by the previous colony. The ship's captain abandoned them there. In August John White left for England to get supplies. When he got there, he found that no ships were available because England was at war with Spain, so he couldn't return to Roanoke Island with the supplies.

1590 - At last the war was over and John White came back to America. He discovered that the colonists were gone. He believed they had found refuge with the Croatoans. The ship returned to England and John White was never able to come back. No one knows for sure what happened to the colony.

1607 - The colony was established at Jamestown. It was about 1650 before people migrated south from Virginia to start settling in North Carolina.

Activities:

1. Make a model of an Algonquian Village. You can find pictures painted by John White in *The American Indian in North Carolina* by Douglas L. Rights.

2. Make a wickiup (or model). See the websites listed below and the pictures by John White. Wickiups were built out of whatever materials were natural to the area. On the coast they were made of grasses over a frame built of wooden poles.

3. Sit in a circle and take turns telling some stories that have been passed down in your family from your grandparents. The Native Americans used a talking feather that was passed around. Whoever held the feather was the only one who could speak. Everyone else had to be silent and listen. When the speaker was finished he/she passed the feather to the next person.

4. Name some foods we enjoy that were gifts from the Native American people. Cornbread, sunflower seeds, prunes and raisins, potatoes, squash, beans, and jerky are a few.

Prepare some of these foods and share them with friends or classmates.

5. Have you ever dreamed you could fly, or do something fantastic? Write a poem or story about your dream.

6. Visit a museum with Native American displays. Notice how baskets were made, how tightly they were woven. What else did you learn about Native American life before the white people came to America?

7. Have you found artifacts like arrowheads or pieces of pottery? Bring them to class for "show and tell." Ask your librarian if you can make a display in the school library. Label the artifacts and put them in a place where they cannot be touched, such as a glass display case or shadow box, which can be purchased at arts and crafts stores.

8. Find the places Gray Squirrel and Heita Hoonoch explored on a North Carolina map. Use the map in the book. Is today's map different than that one? Find a picture of a map drawn in the 16th century. How is it different?

Additional Resources:

An Algonquian Year, The Year According to the Full Moon, by Michael McCurdy. This picture book explains the Native American names of the months, and describes daily life of the Indians.

Horse Follow Closely, by GaWaNi Pony Boy. This book is about training horses by Native American traditional methods. It contains beautiful illustrations and a description of the meaning of symbols that were painted on war horses. This book is about a later time in history than *Pale as the Moon.*

Visit a Pow Wow (first do some research on proper pow wow etiquette).

Websites:

Lumbee Heritage, a documentary by WRAL TV.
www.uncp.edu/lumbeeriverfund.resources.htm

North Carolina Commission of Indian Affairs. This site has
some great fact sheets.
www.doa.state.nc.us/cia/indian.htm

Society of Native American Culture at North Carolina State
University
http://clubs.ncsu.edu/nasa

Frisco Native American Museum
www.nativeamericanmuseum.org/

Biography of John White

www.nps.gov/fora/jwhite.htm

Lost Colony Drama

www.outerbanks.com/lostcolony/60years.htm

Wickiups

www.texasindians.com/wickiup.htm

Wolf Creek Indian Village & Museum in Bastian, Virginia.

www.indianvillage.org

About the Author:

Donna Campbell Smith has an AAS Degree in Equine Technology and Instructor Certificate from Martin Community College. She grew up near the Outer Banks of North Carolina, an area rich in history, natural beauty and home to several bands of wild horses. Donna has combined her knowledge of the horse and child relationship with her interest in the history of coastal North Carolina to write Pale as the Moon.

In addition to Pale as the Moon (Faithful Publishing 2006) Donna Campbell Smith is also the author of An Independent Spirit, to be released by Faithful Publishing at a later date, and The Book of Miniature Horses (The Lyons Press 2005) Her articles and stories appear in several magazines and equine publications.

Donna is available for school author visits and a writer-in-resident program that uses historical fiction to teach the writing process. Programs include writing workshops for all grades, Native Americans of the Carolina Coast, Colonial Carolina and Wild Horses of the Outer Banks.

Visit her website:

http://donnacsmith.tripod.com/

Or contact Donna at:

Donna Campbell Smith
PO Box 1372
Wake Forest, NC 27588

donnacsmith_1@hotmail.com

CPSIA information can be obtained at www.ICGtesting.com
Printed in the USA
LVOW081340190313

324997LV00001B/13/A